The Cat Who Lived with Anne Frank

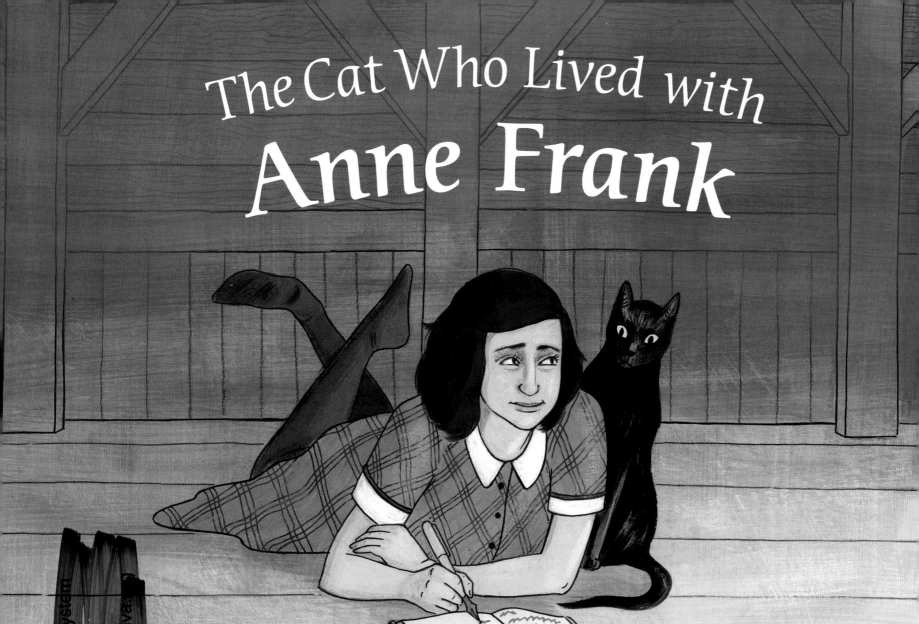

by David Lee Miller and Steven Jay Rubin

illustrated by Elizabeth Baddeley

PHILOMEL BOOKS

My boy Peter gathers me inside his coat. The heavy one with the Yellow Star. He wears layers and layers of clothing even though it's a hot summer day.

I know to stay still, quiet. Because Jews are forbidden to own pets.

I burrow.
I breathe between the
buttons.
I smell the sea, the herring,
the tulips. I hear my boy's shoes
clacking cobblestones.
I hear angry soldiers and
trucks and barking dogs.
The ones with Black
Spiders on their bloodred
armbands, collars, flags
and banners.

Peter's heart quickens.
Mine does too.
Until our hearts beat as one.
Church bells chime over crying gulls and the
watery putt-putt of canal barges.

Suddenly we're inside.
Peter opens his coat, and
a warmhearted woman
scratches my ears.
I gulp delicious air
tingling with spice from
the factory below.

Miep leads us up steep stairs to a bookcase.
A bookcase that opens like magic to a hidden
door and hidden rooms.

A girl is there.

A sparkling, brown-eyed, dark-haired girl. A chatty
Yellow Star girl Peter knows from school. From before the Nazis
and their cruel rules. When we were free and unafraid.

When I rode, kitten face to the wind, perched high in my boy's
speeding bike basket . . . to the Oasis, where Peter snuck me inside
his coat and I licked right from his cone, and the girl giggled, and
she smelled of vanilla too.

Yes, I know this girl.
Her name is Anne. Anne Frank.
The girl smiles a brilliant
smile. She strokes my fur and
says, "Welcome, Mouschi,
to our Secret Annex."

Our hiding place from the Black Spiders is cramped and crowded for eight people and one cat.

Peter and I sleep under the attic stairs.

Anne shares a narrow bedroom
with her sister, Margot. She pastes
up pictures of movie stars, princes,
queens, so it might feel like home.

During the day, when the workers and machines thrum in the spice factory below, we the hidden stay still and silent.

Because if just one of us
steps on a creaky board, sneezes
or knocks a book from a shelf,
someone might hear and know
Yellow Stars are hiding.

And the Black
Spider Soldiers
will come.

Anne passes the difficult days reading and studying. She writes in her red-checkered diary. I curl with Anne as she scribbles and draws and dreams.

I want my diary to be my friend, and I'm going to call this friend Kitty.

Is she talking about me?

Dear Kitty...
Writing in a diary is a really strange experience....
It seems to me later on neither I nor anyone else will be interested in the musings of a thirteen-year-old schoolgirl.

At night, after the spice factory workers are gone, we tiptoe in shadows down through the magic bookcase into the darkened office. The hiders glue to the radio, praying for good news about the war, praying for the Soldiers and Dogs of the Black Spider to leave Holland.

And Anne writes.

We peek from the dark office through thick curtains into the wet night. We see frightened Yellow Stars herded toward the train station. And Anne writes.

Dear Kitty...
I feel wicked sleeping
in a warm bed, while
somewhere out there my
dearest friends are dropping
from exhaustion or being
knocked to the ground.

My job is to give love.

I comfort Anne and Peter when the scary sounds of sirens and falling bombs come too close. They comfort me too when the loud booms rattle the windows.

I hunt the attic rats who steal our precious potatoes and beans. Their itchy insects invade my fur. Peter picks them out, and Anne writes.

I am the only hider who can venture out. I slip through the attic window toward the only glimpse of sky the humans don't veil with black paper, onto the rain gutter, across a chestnut tree.

Anne smiles, wistful, and she writes.

Dear Kitty...
I long to ride a bike,
dance, whistle, look at the world, feel young
and know that I am free,
and yet I can't let it show.

When will we be allowed to breathe fresh air again?

But the streets are far too dangerous for Yellow Stars. Armed Black Spider Soldiers and Dogs patrol, snarl, bark. Roadblocks and checkpoints guard our old Jewish Quarter, Dam Square, every pathway in

I crawl and dash along rooftops.
I'm a shadow in the shadows,
a climber, a leaper.

An explorer, I find hundreds of
Yellow Stars hiding in storage rooms above
the tiger cages at the Artis Zoo, Zookeepers sneaking
them wild animal food while SS Officers picnic and party.

A warrior, I slash and distract Black Spider Dogs as brave Resistance fighters led by a Red-Haired Girl rescue captive Yellow Star babies and children from a hot, smelly prison, once an elegant Jewish Theater.

But I always return to my boy Peter and the girl he now loves.

The girl hiding in the Secret Annex who dreams of being a famous writer someday and touching people's hearts. The girl whose spirit is never broken, even as months turn into years, and Amsterdam is starving.

Dear Kitty...
I still believe,
in spite of everything,
that people are truly
good at heart.

I cuddle with Peter and Anne
on the attic floor. I purr as I feel
the warmth of Anne's heart,
like a fire on a crisp night.
I wonder . . .

Will anybody ever hear my girl's words? Read them?
Wind wisps the chestnut tree towering outside our tiny precious window. Anne whispers, "If we think of all the beauty still around us, we won't give in to sadness."
And to the chestnut's lilt, and the beats and purrs of my boy's and girl's breath, I nap. We nap. Dreaming dreams more powerful than bombs. Dreams of Anne's kind and gentle spirit . . .

lighting up the world forever.

About Anne Frank

Anne was born in Germany. When Adolf Hitler and his Nazis came to power, they banned Jews from going to work or school, destroyed their property, and sometimes even beat and killed them, so Anne and her family moved to Amsterdam. When Anne was ten, Hitler took over Amsterdam, too, and banned Jews from movie theaters and parks, and from using cars and bicycles. Jews couldn't even have pets! And all Jews had to wear a yellow star with *Jood* (Jew) written in black letters.

When the Germans threatened Anne's sister, Margot, the family slipped into hiding in the Secret Annex. Brave friends risked their lives to help the Franks survive. Other friends joined them; a total of eight people hid together, including young Peter, who brought his cat, Mouschi.

For Anne's thirteenth birthday, she was given a checkered red and green diary with a tiny metal lock. She named it Kitty, and in it she wrote about her hopes and dreams.

The people hiding in the Annex were afraid the Nazis would find them. During the day, with workers in the factory below, Anne and the others had to be extremely quiet. Anne longed to be free.

After more than two years of hiding, Nazis found the hidden group and sent them all to concentration camps, where many Jews were forced into labor or killed. Miep, an office worker who had helped hide them, saved Anne's diary. She also rescued Mouschi.

Only Anne's father, Otto, survived. When Miep gave him Anne's diary, Otto read it and cried. Out of the darkness of Otto's grief, the bright light of Anne's words shone through.

Anne's story, spirit and words live on to inspire millions. Anne dreamed about becoming famous, and now she is one of the most famous authors of all time. Today, the house where Anne and Mouschi hid is a museum. You can go see it for yourself.

Some people find it hard to understand the enormous tragedy of the Holocaust. They can't believe the Nazis killed people just because of their religion, race, orientation or circumstances.

But when people read Anne's diary, it becomes real, because they get to know one of the victims personally.

They get to know Anne Frank.

A Note on the Characters and Places in This Story

Mouschi's name for the invading Nazis—the "Black Spiders"—was inspired by the film *The Sound of Music*, in which young Marta von Trapp worries, "Maybe the flag with the Black Spider on it makes people nervous." A cat calling Jews "Yellow Stars" seemed a fine feline fit.

The Red-Haired Girl was a brave Dutch Resistance fighter named Jannetje Johanna Schaft, codenamed "Hannie." The Nazis feared her greatly.

Amsterdam's Jewish Theater was elegant and joyful until the Nazis turned it into a horrific prison and overcrowded deportation center, seizing children from their parents and forcing them into a converted nursery across the street. Hannie and the Resistance heroically smuggled over six hundred of those kids to freedom.

Nazis used Amsterdam's Artis Zoo for their own entertainment, unaware that brave zoo workers were hiding over three hundred Jews in the storage rooms above the cages. There, the Jews sweltered in the summer and froze in the winter, but nearly all of them survived the war.

And, yes, a cat really did live in hiding with Anne Frank. Anne wrote about the cat frequently in her diary.

The cat's name was Mouschi.

Sources

- AnneFrank.org. "The Secret Annex Online." Accessed on December 20, 2017. http://www.annefrank.org/en/Subsites/Home/.
- *The Diary of Anne Frank*. Dir. George Stevens. 20th Century Fox. 1959. Motion picture.
- Frank, Anne. *Anne Frank: The Diary of a Young Girl: The Definitive Edition*. New York: Puffin Books, 2007.
- Frank, Anne. *Anne Frank's Tales from the Secret Annex: A Collection of Her Short Stories, Fables, and Lesser-Known Writings*. New York: Bantam Books, 1982, 2003.
- Gies, Miep, with Alison Leslie Gold. *Anne Frank Remembered: The Story of the Woman Who Helped to Hide the Frank Family*. New York: Simon & Schuster, 1987.
- Gold, Alison Leslie. *Reflections of a Childhood Friend: Memories of Anne Frank*. New York: Scholastic Inc., 1997.
- Hesse, Karen. *Letters from Rifka*. New York: Puffin Books, 1993.
- Lee, Carol Ann. *The Hidden Life of Otto Frank*. New York: William Morrow, 2002.
- Lewis, Brenda Ralph. *The Story of Anne Frank*. London: Dorling Kindersley, 2001.
- Metselaar, Menno, and Ruud van der Rol. *Anne Frank: Her Life in Words and Pictures from the Archives of the Anne Frank House*. Translated by Arnold J. Pomerans. New York: Roaring Book Press, 2009.
- Sawyer, Kem Knapp. *Anne Frank: A Photographic Story of a Life*. London: Dorling Kindersley, 2004.
- "Zoo refuge: Amsterdam menagerie hid Jews from the Nazis." Published on May 10, 2008; accessed on December 20, 2017. https://www.youtube.com/watch?v=HWq5te1jjSM.

PHILOMEL BOOKS
an imprint of Penguin Random House LLC
375 Hudson Street, New York, NY 10014

Library of Congress Cataloging-in-Publication Data
Names: Miller, David Lee, 1955– author. | Rubin, Steven Jay, 1951– author. | Baddeley, Elizabeth,
illustrator. | Title: The cat who lived with Anne Frank / David Lee Miller and Steven Jay Rubin ;
illustrated by Elizabeth Baddeley. | Description: New York, NY : Philomel Books, [2019]
Summary: Mouschi the cat relates the experiences of Anne Frank and seven other people who hid
from Nazis in a secret annex over a factory in Amsterdam during the Holocaust. Includes facts about
the Holocaust and about Anne Frank. | Includes bibliographical references.
Identifiers: LCCN 2018007249 | ISBN 9781524741501 (hardcover) | ISBN 9781524741532 (e-book)
Subjects: | CYAC: Cats—Fiction. | Frank, Anne, 1929–1945—Fiction. | Jews—Netherlands—
Fiction. | Holocaust, Jewish (1939–1945)—Netherlands—Amsterdam—Fiction.
Classification: LCC PZ7.1.M5653 Cat 2019 | DDC [E]—dc23
LC record available at https://lccn.loc.gov/2018007249

Manufactured in China by RR Donnelley Asia Printing Solutions Ltd.
ISBN 9781524741501
10 9 8 7 6 5 4 3 2 1

Edited by Talia Benamy.   Design by Jennifer Chung.
Text set in Breughel.   The art was done in ink, acrylic, pencil and digital.

For children everywhere facing hate
and intolerance—may your lives be
filled with the peace, love and
freedom Anne Frank so cherished.
—**DLM** and **SJR**

For my Mouschi, Harry.
—**EB**